KU-428-845

Dear
L...
...ndpa xxx
Christmas 2015

My Favourite Fairy Tales

© 2014 Brown Watson, England
ISBN: 978 0 7097 2204 5
English edition
Printed in Spain
Reprinted 2015

Illustrator: Javier Inaraja
Graphic Designer: Marcela Grez

© SUSAETA EDICIONES, S.A.
C/ Campezo, 13 - 28022 Madrid
Tel : 91 3009115 - Fax: 91 3009110

This book belongs to

_____

_____

Brown Watson
ENGLAND LE8 0HG

PROLOGUE

This book contains the most wonderful stories ever told. Stories filled with adventure and fantasy; tales of love and beauty, humour and excitement, whose characters have filled the minds of children with magic and illusion.

Tales that have been told for generations are brought to life in this delightful collection. Let children's imaginations soar as you enter this magical world…

SNOW WHITE

In a faraway land there lived a beautiful princess named Snow White. The Queen, her stepmother, was very vain and hated Snow White.

The stepmother would ask her magic mirror,
'Mirror, mirror, who is the fairest in the kingdom?'
'You are the fairest,' the mirror always replied.
But one day the mirror answered, 'Princess Snow
White is the fairest in the kingdom.'

The Queen, full of rage and jealousy, gave orders to her huntsman. 'Take Snow White out into the forest, kill her, and bring me her heart.' But the huntsman felt sorry for her, and let her escape. To deceive the Queen, he gave her the heart of a wild boar.

Snow White ran through the woods, frightened and lost. When morning came, she found a little house and ran towards it. The door was open and there was a little table inside, with seven little chairs and, on the table, seven little plates and seven little spoons.

She ate, and then went up to the bedroom, where she found seven little beds. She lay down and fell fast asleep.

When the owners of the house returned, they were astonished to find her there.

They were seven dwarves who worked in the mine.
Snow White told them her sad story, and the dwarves
invited her to stay with them.

'Thank you,' said Snow
White. 'I will take care
of you and not be
a burden.' The
dwarves loved
their new friend.

But the magic mirror had revealed to the wicked Queen that Snow White was still alive in the forest.

The Queen disguised herself and, finding Snow White alone, she took advantage and offered her a poisoned apple.

As soon as the girl took a bite, she fell senseless to the ground.

When the dwarves came home from the mine, they found Snow White on the ground, pale and quiet, as if she was dead. They put her in a beautiful glass coffin and began to cry.

Before long, a handsome prince came by, and the dwarves told him the girl's story.

The Prince, seeing how beautiful she was, fell in love with her. He kissed her, and the girl came back to life, to the surprise and delight of the dwarves. Soon afterwards, the Prince and Snow White married and lived happily ever after.

LITTLE RED RIDING HOOD

Near a forest lived a pretty, happy little girl, whom everybody loved. They called her Little Red Riding Hood because she always wore a little red cape that her mother had made for her.

One day, her mother said, 'Darling daughter, your grandmother is ill. Take her this basket with cheese, cake and a jar of honey. And be careful. Don't go through the forest or speak to any strangers.'

Little Red Riding Hood put on her hood and said goodbye to her mother. She was feeling very brave so decided to take a short cut through the forest. She went along happily, saying hello to all the little animals that she met.

Suddenly, a wolf sprang out from behind a tree. But Little Red Riding Hood was not easily frightened. She greeted him, 'Good morning, Mr Wolf.'

'Where are you going, Little Red Riding Hood?' asked the wolf.

'I'm going to see my poorly grandmother who lives just on the other side of the forest. I'm sorry but I really should hurry to her. Goodbye Mr Wolf.'

The wolf said goodbye and scampered off along a shortcut to the cottage.

The wolf ran as fast as he could to the grandmother's house and knocked at the door.

'Who's there?' the old lady asked.

'It's me, Little Red Riding Hood,' the wolf answered, imitating the little girl's voice.

The hungry wolf burst in. When the old lady saw that it was not her granddaughter, she ran as fast as she could and hid in the closet! The wolf did not care. He was happy to wait for Little Red Riding Hood to appear so he could eat them both together!

When the little girl arrived, she was surprised to find the door open. 'Grandmother, it's me!' she called and entered the little house.

She placed her basket on the bed and then gasped.
'Grandmother, grandmother, what big ears you have!'
'All the better to hear you with,' squeaked the wolf.
'Grandmother, grandmother, what big eyes you have!'
'All the better to see you with,' he replied.

'Grandmother, grandmother, what big teeth you have!'

'All the better to eat you with!' the wolf roared, racing after Little Red Riding Hood. He snapped his mighty jaws at her ankles.

Little Red Riding Hood ran as fast as she could!
Luckily, some woodcutters heard the commotion
and ran to help. They tied up the wolf and took
him away. Little Red Riding Hood ran back to the
cottage where her grandmother was still hiding,
very frightened!

Little Red Riding Hood and her grandmother hugged each other tightly. Together they sat at the edge of the forest, happy that the wolf had done them no harm. But Little Red Riding Hood's grandmother made sure that the girl had learnt her lesson. Now she knows how important it is not to talk to strangers, and to always listen to her mother...

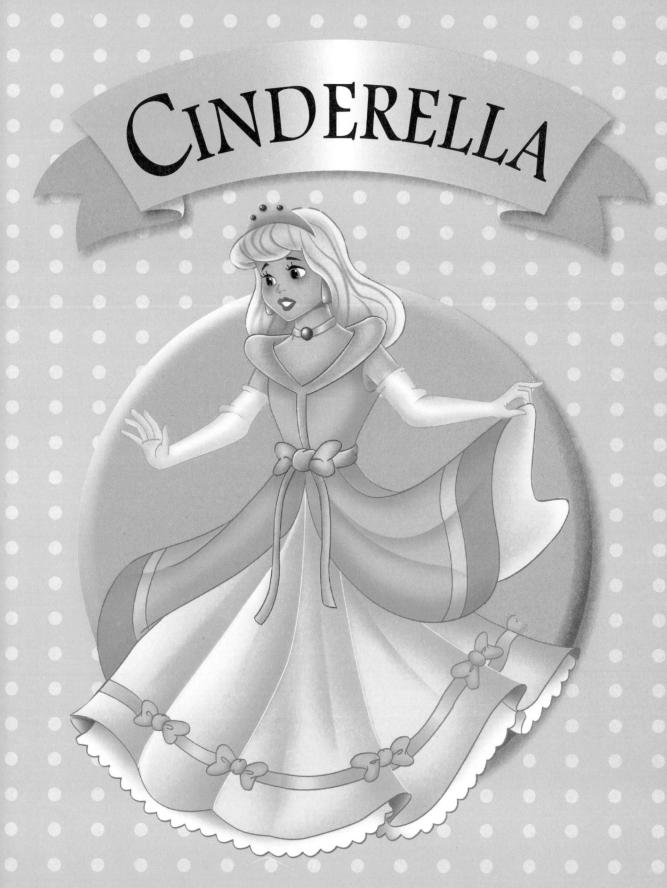

CINDERELLA

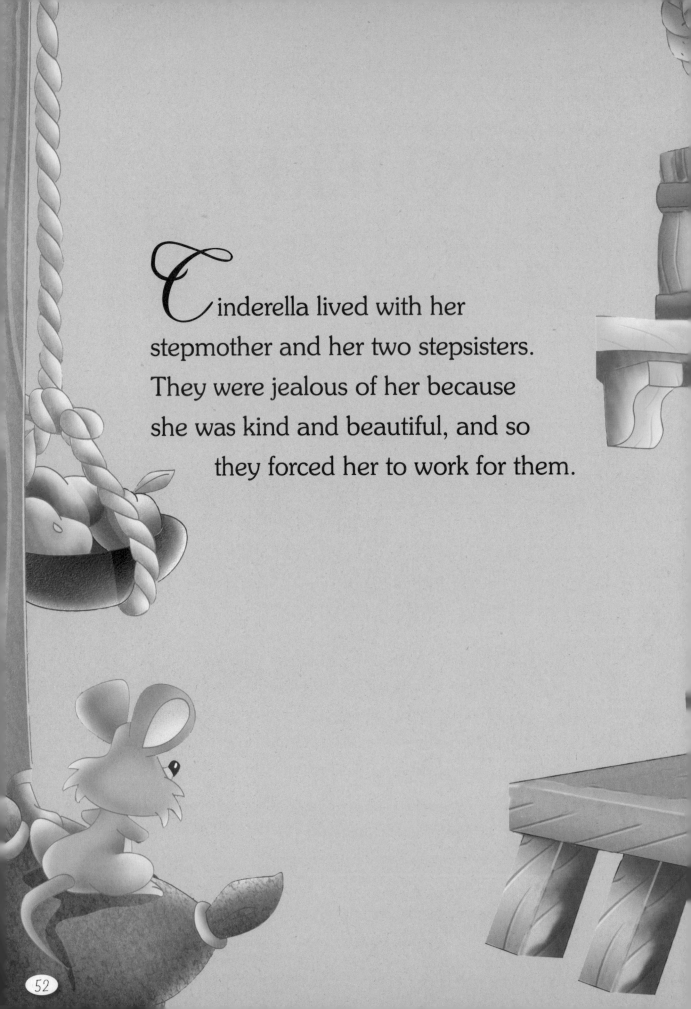

Cinderella lived with her stepmother and her two stepsisters. They were jealous of her because she was kind and beautiful, and so they forced her to work for them.

One day they were invited to a ball that the Prince was holding at the palace, but Cinderella was not allowed to go. She watched sadly as her stepmother and stepsisters dressed up and headed to the ball.
                    She so wished she could join them.

Cinderella was left feeling very sad.
Suddenly her fairy godmother appeared
and said, 'You are very good, and you
deserve to go to the ball!'

With her magic wand, she turned the ragged clothes into a wonderful dress. With another wave of her wand, she changed a pumpkin into a coach, and some mice into horses and elegant coachmen.

'One thing you must keep in mind,' the fairy told her. 'You must come home before midnight, as that is when the spell will break.'

Cinderella left for the ball at once.

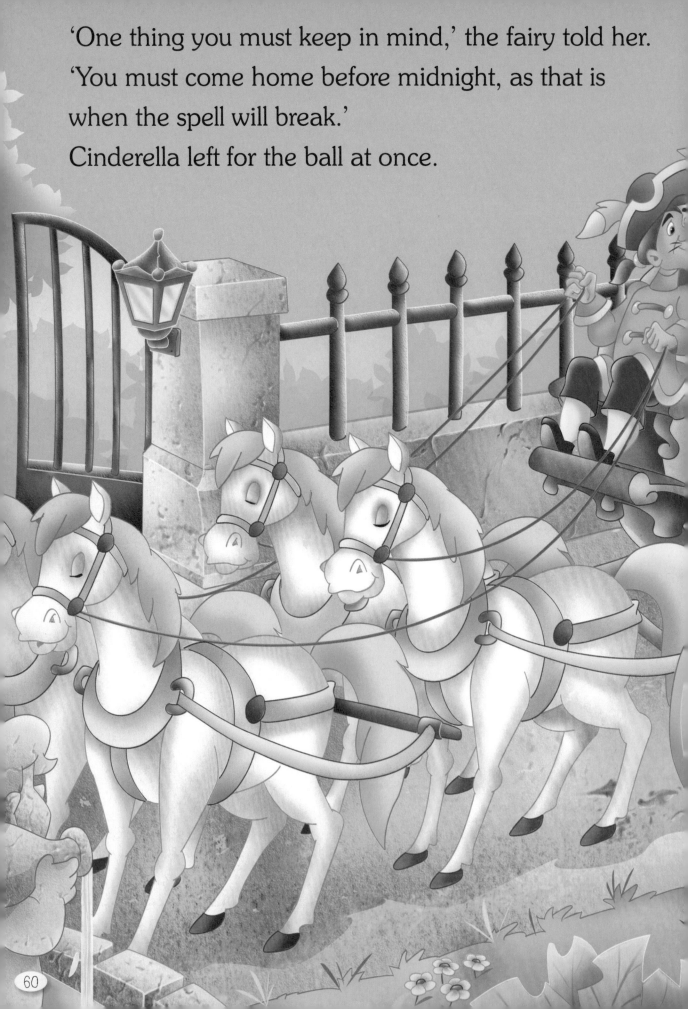

At the ball, the Prince only had eyes for her. They danced together all night long. The guests agreed that they made a beautiful couple. Everyone was wondering who this young woman was, since not even her stepmother or her stepsisters recognised her.

Cinderella was so happy that she only remembered her fairy godmother's warning when she heard the first chime of the clock striking twelve. She left the palace in such a hurry that she lost one of her glass slippers.

Since all that he had left of her was the glass slipper, the Prince announced that he would marry the girl to whom the slipper belonged. He went through the whole kingdom trying it on all the ladies, but nobody had feet as small as Cinderella's.

Cinderella tried the slipper,
and it fitted her foot perfectly.
The Prince and Cinderella were
very happy to see each other
again, and promised that they
would never be separated.

THE LITTLE MERMAID

$\mathcal{M}$any years ago, there lived at the bottom of the sea a mermaid who was very beautiful; however, she felt very unhappy because they would not let her visit the surface. She longed to see what life was like on the shore.

One night she could no longer contain her
curiosity, and without being seen by anybody,
she rose to the surface to admire the wonders
of the land.

The sea was very rough, and the little mermaid saw a ship being wrecked on the reef.

A young man was struggling in the waves, calling for help. She swam to him, lifted him and kept him from drowning. But he had fainted and could not see that it was the little mermaid who had saved him.

The little mermaid kept him afloat and pulled him to the beach. She did not want him to see her mermaid's tail.

From the rocks, she watched some men pick up the young man, who turned out to be a Prince.

The little mermaid, in love with the Prince, took a potion that the Witch of the Sea gave her. In return for her voice, it turned her tail into legs.

The Prince found the little mermaid on the beach.
Of course, he did not recognise her, and the little
mermaid had no voice to tell him who she was. On the
following day, the Prince gave a ball at the palace and
invited the little mermaid. She accepted with delight.

At the ball, the Prince introduced her to his fiancée. The little mermaid was desperately sad and ran off towards the sea.

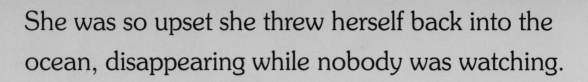

She was so upset she threw herself back into the ocean, disappearing while nobody was watching.

Luckily, Neptune, the King of the Sea, was able to give her back her tail, and the little mermaid became as she had been before.

Since then, on the night of the full moon, accompanied by dolphins and seagulls, the little mermaid watches the ships and fondly remembers her beloved Prince.

ALADDIN

*L*ong ago, in an Eastern city, lived a humble tailor with his wife and son, Aladdin.

Aladdin's father died and so the boy had to find work in order to support himself and his poor mother. One day, a wizard came to the city. He offered to pay Aladdin a small fortune if he would go with him to a very mysterious place. Aladdin thought of his hungry mother and decided to accompany the wizard, thinking of all the food he could buy with the money.

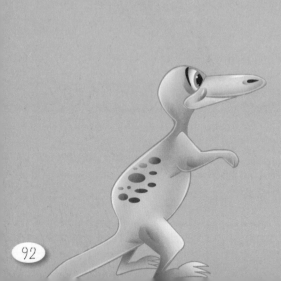

The wizard took Aladdin outside the city, to a deserted town near the mountains. 'What a spooky place!' Aladdin thought.

The wizard shouted a magic spell, and with a terrible roar the earth opened! The wizard commanded Aladdin to climb down into the cave below. He told him he would find vast amounts of jewels and treasure, but he must look carefully for a golden lamp.

Aladdin started to search through the mountains of precious treasure and filled his pockets with as much as he could. The wizard shouted nervously, 'You are only allowed to touch the lamp! I want you to bring it to me!' But Aladdin was fascinated at what was before his eyes, and no longer listened to the wizard. Slowly, the cave's entrance closed and left Aladdin searching through the treasure alone.

Aladdin picked up the lamp the wizard had mentioned. There were a few dusty marks on it, so he rubbed it to make it clean. Suddenly a genie appeared! 'O master! I am your genie; ask me whatever you want!' it cried.

Aladdin had always wanted to become a prince and so hesitantly he asked the genie. The genie granted his wish and Aladdin married a beautiful princess.

The wizard was angry at Aladdin. He wanted the magic lamp for himself. He pretended to be a trader and visited the palace when Aladdin was away. The wizard persuaded one of the maids to sell him Aladdin's lamp. He laughed wickedly, and rubbed the lamp hard. When the genie appeared, the wizard ordered him to bring all of the riches Aladdin had, including his palace.

Upon hearing what had happened,
Aladdin pulled out a magic ring he
had found in the cave. He rubbed it
and another genie appeared. 'Bring
my riches and my palace back to me!'

He continued, 'Then send the evil wizard to a place far, far away where he can do no harm to anyone!' The genie made his wishes come true. Aladdin recovered all their wealth and was able to live in his majestic palace again.

Aladdin and his Princess were happy again, and Aladdin soon became king. Now the two genies are great friends, and help Aladdin to rule with fairness and kindness.

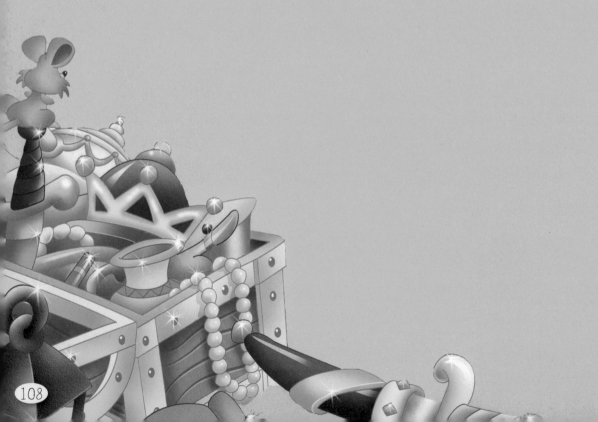

PINOCCHIO

One day, a poor toymaker
called Gepetto made a beautiful puppet.
Gepetto decided to call the puppet
Pinocchio. To Gepetto's astonishment,
the puppet began to talk and move, just
like a real boy!

The next day, Gepetto bought Pinocchio a
satchel and some books, and sent him to school,
accompanied by a cricket. On the way to school
Pinocchio saw a puppet theatre and, despite the
cricket's advice, Pinocchio danced and sang on the
stage with the other puppets.

The owner of the puppet theatre wanted to keep Pinocchio, but the poor puppet cried so much that he gave him some coins and let him go.

On his way home, Pinocchio met
a fox and a cat, who were both thieves.
The cricket warned Pinocchio not to go with the thieves,
but he ignored his advice. They took him to a place they
called the Field of Miracles and told him to bury his coins
in order to become very rich.

Pinocchio did as he was told, but the thieves
tied him up and stole his coins. The animals
helped to rescue him and a dove told him
that Gepetto had gone to look for him at sea.

A kind fairy took pity on Pinocchio and took him home. She told him to be a good boy, and warned him:

'Every time you tell a lie, your nose will grow. You must go and find Gepetto, he is out searching for you and is extremely worried!'

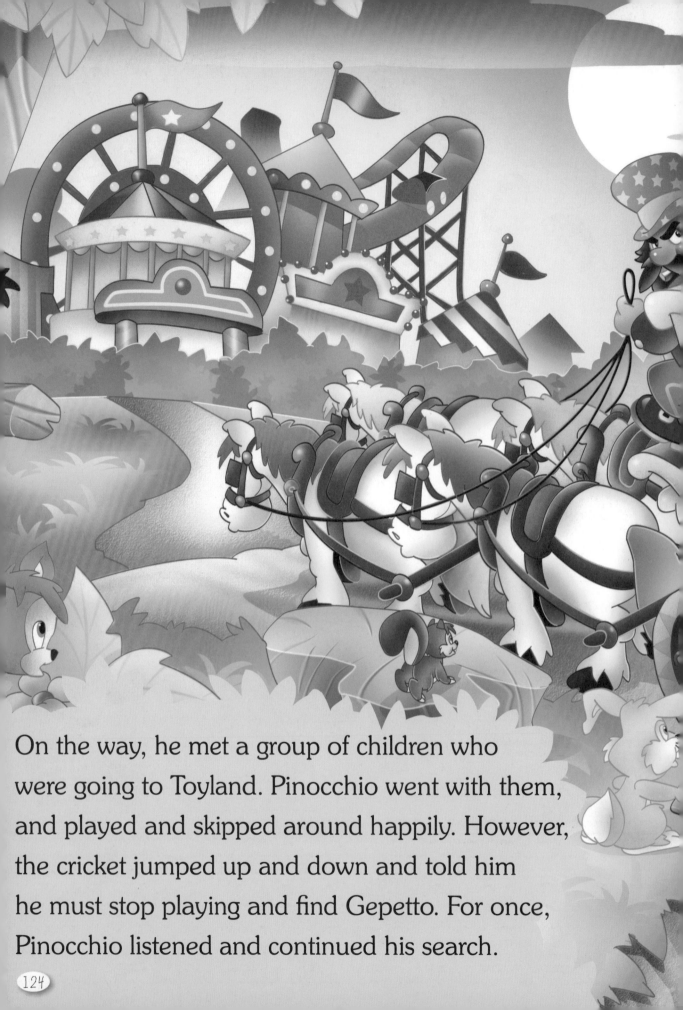

On the way, he met a group of children who were going to Toyland. Pinocchio went with them, and played and skipped around happily. However, the cricket jumped up and down and told him he must stop playing and find Gepetto. For once, Pinocchio listened and continued his search.

Pinocchio and the cricket left for the sea in search of Gepetto. Imagine their surprise when they were swallowed by a huge whale, and found Gepetto in the whale's stomach! Luckily, the whale yawned, and all three of them were able to escape through his huge mouth.

When they reached the shore safe and
sound, the fairy turned Pinocchio into
a real boy as he had been so good
and brave. From that day forwards,
he always behaved himself.

BAMBI

All the animals of the forest came together to celebrate the birth of Bambi, the little fawn, son of the Great Prince of the Forest. It was the beginning of a springtime full of adventures.

The rabbit Thumper took young Bambi to meet
all the animals of the forest.
'Look, Bambi, a bird!' Thumper would say.
'Bird!' Bambi would repeat.

The winter arrived and the forest was covered in snow. Bambi struggled to keep his balance on the ice. The animals had fun throwing snowballs at each other.

Faline, a doe the same age as Bambi, played with them too.

But one day, the hunters appeared in the wood, mercilessly firing their guns. The terrified animals fled in all directions.

'Run away, my son, don't stop!' Bambi's mother called him. But the hunters fired, and she fell, lifeless, into the snow.

All the animals mourned her loss and tried to console little Bambi. His father, the Great Prince of the Forest, came to him and said, 'The men killed your mother. From now on, I will protect you.'

When spring arrived, Bambi had grown a great deal. He had fine antlers and had learned all his father taught him.

One day he met a beautiful doe. 'Hello, Bambi!' she said. 'Don't you recognise me anymore?' It was Faline, who, like him, had grown up and had become a beautiful young creature.

All the animals were distracted with the
happiness of the new spring when, suddenly,
a curtain of fire sprang up on the horizon.

Bambi ran through the forest, warning all the others. 'Everyone go to the island in the river!' he shouted. Together with his father, he saved many animals who could not have crossed the water by themselves.

Thanks to Bambi and
his father, all the animals
escaped to safety. In time,
Bambi became the Great
Prince of the Forest and
he and Faline lived happily
together with all their loyal
forest friends.

HANSEL AND GRETEL

Hansel and Gretel were brother and sister, and they lived in a cottage in the woods.

Their parents were poor woodcutters, and did not know how they could feed their children. They decided to leave them to fend for themselves.

In the morning, their father took them into the forest. 'Stay here and pick up the firewood we have cut. I'll come back for you in a little while,' he said.

But night fell and their
parents did not return, so
Hansel and Gretel decided to
look for the way home.

All the trees of the forest looked the same to
them, and they ended up getting lost.

They were sleepy and hungry. They walked all
night, until they finally fell asleep under a tree.
When morning dawned, while they carried
on searching for the way home, Hansel found
something. 'Look, Gretel!' It was a house made
of sweets, with a roof
of chocolate.

The walls were made of gingerbread, the windows of sugar and the door was made of caramel. They ran to it and began to gobble the sweet things. Suddenly the owner of the house appeared: an old lady who invited them in.

Once inside, the old lady, who was really a witch, thrust Hansel into a cage and made Gretel do her chores. She forced them to eat more sweet things. 'When you get fat enough, I'll eat you!' cackled the witch.

'Listen, children! Today is my five hundredth birthday, and I've decided to celebrate it with a special meal: Hansel, you'll be the main course!' the witch cackled, while Hansel and Gretel listened in terror.

While the witch prepared the food, she made Gretel light the oven so she could cook her brother. Gretel knew she had to obey or the witch would turn her into a frog. Then she would never be able to save her brother.

'Now the oven is hot, it's time to pop you in there!' laughed the witch. She unlocked the cage and pulled Hansel out.

Quick as a flash, Hansel jumped out of the cage and pushed the witch with all his strength. He shoved her into the open oven and slammed the door. Hansel danced for joy. 'We're free!' he cried.

They found a chest of gold coins under the witch's bed and took it with them. The witch owned a magic goose, which carried the children safely through the forest and back to their cottage. Their parents were so happy to see them! From that day onwards, they all lived happily ever after.

THE THREE LITTLE PIGS

$\mathcal{I}$n a little house in the forest, three little pigs lived happily with their parents. Since they were now fully grown, they decided that each would build his own house to live in.

The first little pig, the laziest in the family, decided to build himself a house of straw. In a moment his hut was built, and he sat back to rest.

The second little pig, who
was very greedy, built a house
of wood. He threw it together
quickly, and then sat down for
a snack.

The third little pig, who was the hardest worker, built a house of bricks and mortar. It took him a long time to build it, but he made a safe and very handsome house.

Not long afterwards, the hungry wolf approached the first little pig's cabin. 'Open the door, or I'll huff, and I'll puff, and I'll blow your house down!'

The little pig did not open the door, so the wolf huffed and puffed, and the house of straw blew away. The little pig, extremely frightened, ran to hide in his brother's house.

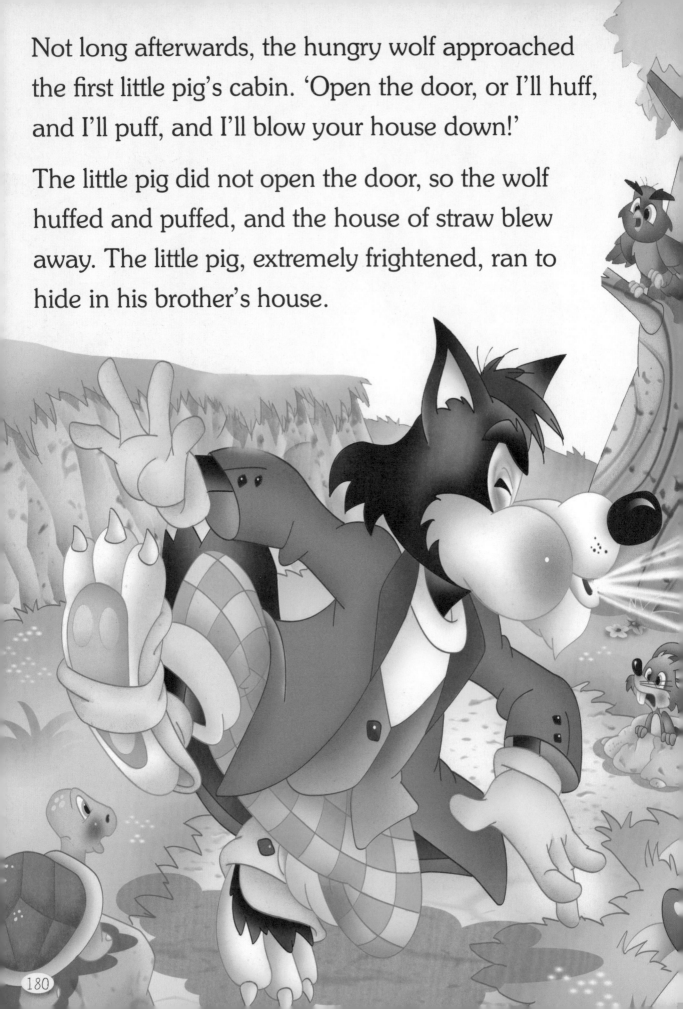

The wolf followed him and knocked at the second door. 'Open the door, or I'll blow your house down!'

This little pig would not open the door either, so the wolf huffed and puffed, and the hut fell apart. Terrified, the two little pigs ran to their brother's house.

The wolf knocked at the door, and shouted, 'Open the door, or I'll huff, and I'll puff, and I'll blow your house down!' The first two little pigs were terrified.

'Blow all you want, but I won't open the door!' said the little pig. The wolf huffed and puffed with all his might, but the house didn't move.

The wolf climbed onto the roof and slid down the chimney. The little pigs put a cauldron of water on to boil, and the wolf fell in.

With his tail scalded, he ran away and never came back. The little pigs lived happily together in the house made of bricks by the clever, hard working brother.

THE UGLY DUCKLING

Once upon a time there was a duck who had four beautiful little ducklings, but when the last one broke out of his egg…

'Oh! What an ugly duckling!'

When the mother duck took her children swimming, all the farmyard animals would look at them and laugh. 'Good heavens! Poor duck, he is so ugly!' His brothers and sisters were ashamed of him. 'Go away! It's your fault that everyone is staring at us!'

The poor duckling moved so far away from them that he ended up on the opposite bank. Then some shots rang out, and the ugly duckling saw a flock of geese taking flight. The hunters' dogs saw the duckling and chased him.

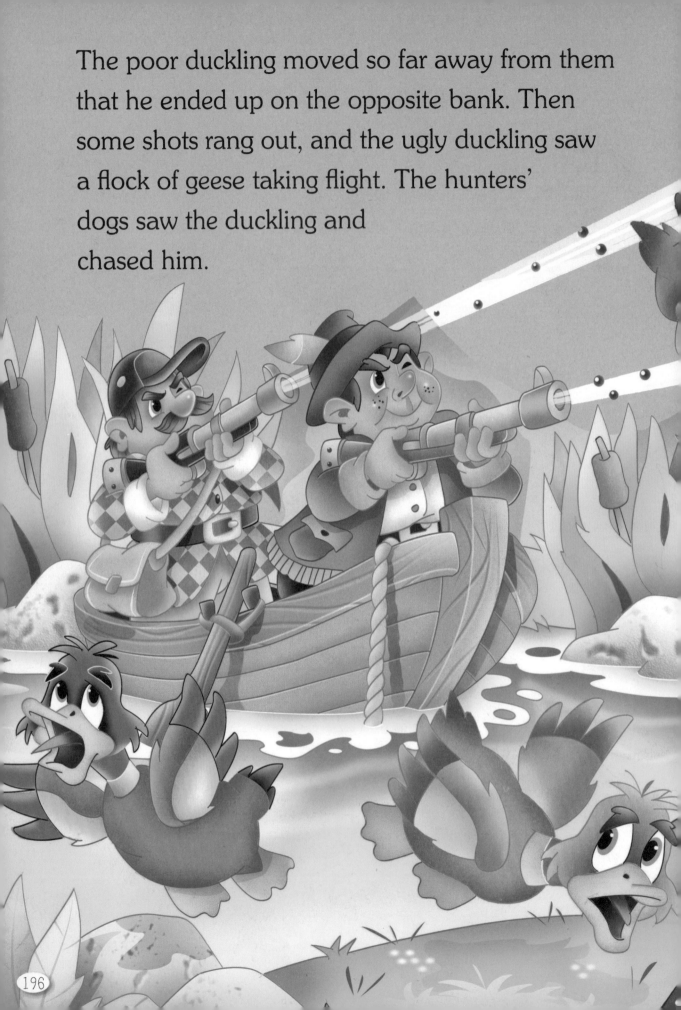

He managed to escape them, but since he had nowhere to go, he kept on walking. Then winter came....

The animals of the forest watched him with pity, seeing how cold he was.

199

It snowed and snowed. The duckling hid in an old tree trunk, where he was found by an old woman and her dog.

'Poor little thing! How ugly and thin he is!' said the woman, and took him home with her.

She took good care of him, and he was very happy. Everyone liked him…except the jealous cat. 'Since that duck arrived, nobody pays me any attention,' he thought.

Spring arrived. The jealous cat had had enough of the duckling, and chased him out of the house. The old woman was sad, but could not get the duckling back. The poor duckling wandered for weeks with nowhere to live.

He arrived at a lake, where there were two beautiful swans. The duckling thought that they would peck at him. Frightened, he was going to hide his head under his wing when he suddenly saw a beautiful swan reflected in the water – it was none other than himself!

The swans took flight, and the ugly duckling took off into the skies with them. As they passed over his old farm, the animals looked up at the sky and exclaimed, 'Look at the swans! How beautiful and graceful they are!' The ugly duckling felt truly happy for the first time.

PUSS IN BOOTS

There was once a poor miller who, when he died, left to his three sons his mill, his donkey, and, to the youngest, his cat.

The miller's son was unhappy with his small inheritance, but the cat told him not to be sad. He promised that he would make him rich.

The cat asked his master to find him some boots and a sack.

When he had them, the cat ran out in search of the King's palace.

On the way, the cat hunted a rabbit and presented it to the King, on behalf of his master, the Marquis of Carabas. The King thanked him.

The cat continued for two or three months, bringing hunting trophies to the King, always as a gift from his master.

One day, the cat knew that the King would be passing by the river with his beautiful daughter. He told his master to bathe in the river, and said he had a plan. When the King passed, the cat came running out, crying, 'Help, help! My master, the Marquis of Carabas, is drowning!'

They helped to rescue him and
the King invited the Marquis of
Carabas to accompany him
on his journey. The cat
ran ahead of the royal
coach and horses.

He warned all the peasants he met along the way: 'When the King's coach passes by, tell him that these lands belong to the Marquis of Carabas.'

The cat arrived at a castle, which belonged to an ogre, together with the lands. The ogre received him courteously.

'They tell me,' said the cat, 'that you have the power to turn yourself into any animal – a lion, for example.'

The ogre turned into a fierce lion. 'But I'm sure you cannot turn into a small animal, like a mouse.'

Sure enough, the ogre turned into a little mouse and began to run along the ground. The moment he saw him, the clever cat pounced on him and ate him in a single mouthful.

The royal coach pulled up outside. 'Welcome to the home of the Marquis of Carabas,' said the cat, and invited them to visit the castle.

The King was so delighted by the qualities and the riches of the Marquis that he offered him the hand of the beautiful Princess in marriage.

The Marquis and the
Princess were married.
The cat became a great
lord, and he never had
to chase another mouse,
except for fun.

The Wolf and the Seven Little Goats

Mother Goat lived in a little house in the forest with her seven children. One day she had to go to the market, and she warned her little ones:

'Beware of the wolf and don't open the door; if you open it, he'll eat you.'

Soon afterwards, the wolf knocked at the door of the house. He said in his sweetest voice, 'Open the door for me, children, it's Mother!'

But the little goats saw the wolf's dark coat. 'No, you're not our mother! Go away, you bad wolf!' the bravest little goat replied.

The cunning wolf waited for the miller to pass by, and covered his paws in flour. He went and knocked again at the door, and showed them one paw. He tricked the little goats, and they opened the door, thinking he was their mother.

The wolf leaped on them and ate them up one by one without chewing, so as to eat them as quickly as possible.

Only the smallest escaped, by hiding in the old grandfather clock. That was where his mother found him when she came home. He was so happy to see her again.

The mother goat took scissors, a needle and thread, and she and her little one went in search of the wolf. With his belly full, he had laid down on the riverbank for a snooze.

The mother goat cut open the wolf's stomach with her scissors, and the little goats came out safe and happy. Then they filled his stomach with stones, and the mother goat sewed it shut again.

'How thirsty I am!' roared the wolf when he woke up, and he approached the riverbank to take a drink. But the stones that filled his stomach were so heavy that he fell into the river and drowned.

And from that day on, the mother goat and her little goats had a peaceful and happy life, with no wolf coming to trouble them.

My favourite story was

_____

_____

_____

because _____

_____

_____

_____

_____

_____

_____

_____

My favourite character is

_____

_____

_____

because _____

_____

_____

_____

_____

_____

_____

INDEX OF STORIES